DINO DOG

Jane Clarke

Illustrated by Garry Parsons

CORGI PUPS

D0994737

For Val and Mike. Thanks, mates!

DINO DOG
A CORGI PUPS BOOK : 9780552550321

Published in Great Britain by Corgi Books,
an imprint of Random House Children's Publishers UK

This edition published 2004

9 10 8

The Random House Group Limited supports The Forest Stewardship
Council® (FSC®), the leading international forest-certification organisation.
Our books carrying the FSC label are printed on FSC®-certified paper.
FSC is the only forest-certification scheme supported by the leading
environmental organisations, including Greenpeace. Our
paper procurement policy can be found at
www.randomhouse.co.uk/environment

MIX
Paper from
responsible sources
FSC® C016897

Set in 18/25pt Bembo Schoolbook

Corgi Pups Books are published by Random House Children's Publishers UK
61–63 Uxbridge Road, London W5 5SA,
A Random House Group Company

Addresses for companies within The Random House Group Limited
can be found at: www.randomhouse.co.uk/offices.htm

THE RANDOM HOUSE GROUP Limited Reg. No. 954009
www.randomhousechildrens.co.uk

A CIP catalogue record for this book is available from the British Library.

Printed and bound in Great Britain by
Clays Ltd, St Ives plc

Contents

Series Reading Consultant: Prue Goodwin
Lecturer in Literacy and Children's Books, University of Reading

Contents

Chapter One

"Come here!"

The dog scuttled along the beach as fast as his stubby little legs would carry him.

"I wish you two would keep him under control," Mum said.

"We're trying to," said David.
"It will be easier when we know
his name."

"Why don't you give him a
new name? It's ages since we
got him from the Rescue
Centre."

"He's lost his home and his family," said Lucy. "He can't lose his name as well. We have to keep trying different names until we find the right one."

"Sandy!" yelled David. "Come here!"

The dog accelerated away, kicking up a shower of pebbles.

"Oh, no!" Mum said. "He's running towards that woman. I hope he doesn't jump up . . ."

"Get him off me!"

David and Lucy ran and grabbed the dog's collar. The woman brushed wet sandy pawprints from the front of her tweed skirt.

"Sorry," Lucy said.

Mum ran up, panting. "I'm very sorry, Mrs . . ."

"Miss Stone."

"He's only being friendly," Lucy said. "This sort of dog likes people."

"What sort of dog? He looks like a fat hairy sausage."

"He's a spanoodle," said David.

"A cross between a spaniel and a poodle," Lucy explained.

"With a bit of Jack Russell and dachshund thrown in," said Mum.

The dog rolled over onto his back and kicked his legs in the air.

"He wants you to tickle his tummy," David said.

"I must be getting on." Miss Stone adjusted her backpack.

"These fossils are heavy."

"What have you found?" asked Lucy.

"Fossilized wood from the beach back there. The Isle of Wight's a great place to find fossils. I'm always hoping to find something special to add to my collection." Miss Stone turned and wandered off towards the base of the cliffs.

The dog jumped to his feet and shoved his nose into a heap of pebbles. His stumpy tail wagged wildly.

"So, Pebbles," Lucy said. "You like stones, do you?"

The dog turned his back on Lucy and dropped a stone at David's feet. Beneath the slimy slobber was the imprint of a spiral shell.

"It's an ammonite!" David said. "Clever boy, you found a fossil!"

Chapter Two

The dog shot off like a rocket.

"Flash!" David yelled. "Come back!"

The dog skidded to a halt at the base of the cliffs. He began to scrabble at the crumbly mudstone.

"Scrabble! Come here!" Lucy called. The dog began to dig. "If we knew his name," David said, "he might take some notice of us."

"COME HERE, DIGGER!" they shouted. No response.

"He's found something," said David. "Let's go and have a look."

"Careful," Mum said. "These cliffs are dangerous."

They scrunched up the
beach. The dog stopped digging.
His nose was covered in mud.
Something was wedged in his
mouth.

"Good boy!" David said. He
took a chocolate bar out of his
pocket. It was half-melted and
covered in fluff and sand.

"Look what I've got . . . Would you like some?"

Pttth! The dog spat out what was in his mouth and grabbed the chocolate bar.

"What is it?" asked Lucy, looking at the dark grey triangular-shaped object the dog had dropped.

"I can't tell. It's too slobbery."

"It's only a pebble." Mum prodded it with her foot. "Let's go back to the caravan. It's time to eat."

"I think it's another fossil."
David picked up the stone and
wiped it on his T-shirt. "It looks
like a tooth."

"Miss Stone's coming back
towards us," said Lucy.

"She'll know
what it is."

"Has he
found
something?"
Miss Stone
asked. "May I see?"
David handed her the
damp object.

Miss Stone turned it over in her hand and looked at it closely. Her eyes lit up. "A lucky find, but not a rare one," she said quickly, not meeting David's eye. "It's a fossilized shark's tooth. I have several in my collection." She handed it back to David.

"If you take my advice, you'll look on the beach rather than in these dangerous cliffs. They're very unstable after the recent storms. There could be a landslip at any time." She hitched up the straps of her backpack and waved them farewell.

"You found a tooth! Clever boy, Fang!" Lucy said.

The dog ignored her and pawed hopefully at David.

"Chocolate's bad for dogs," David said. "Go and see if you can find some more fossils."

The dog began to snuffle around. "Is your name Fossil?" David asked.

"Miss Stone's right," Mum said. "This cliff isn't safe. That's a new rock fall. You can see where it broke off." She pointed to a scar in the cliff.

The dog looked up.

"*Ruff!* . . ."

"What are you barking at?" Lucy asked. "There's nothing there."

"*Ruff, ruff, ruff!*"

The dog pawed at the scar in the cliff. Small pieces of mudstone pattered to the ground.

"Stop him!" Mum said. "He'll start a landslip!"

David grabbed the dog's collar. "Look! There's something sticking out of the rock," he said.

"It's only a stick," said Lucy.

The dog hurled himself at the cliff and grabbed the stick. His feet swung backwards and forwards as he hung on.

Thlupp. The stick came free from the cliff and the dog landed in a heap.

"You got it, Gripper!" David said. "Now let go!"

David grasped one end of the stick and lifted it up. The dog's teeth slid down it and he fell off the end.

"No wonder you couldn't  hang on," said David. "This isn't a stick, it's a bone! A fossilized bone!"

Chapter Three

"There's not much space in this caravan," said Mum, "but I've managed to cook us a proper meal. Fish fingers, mashed potatoes, carrots and spinach."

David pulled a face. "After we've finished eating," he said, "we can go and see if there are any more fossil bones in the cliff." He squirted tomato ketchup on his fish fingers.

"No, we can't!" Mum put down her knife and fork. "The cliffs are too dangerous."

"I want to find out what the bone is from," Lucy said.

"Someone at the museum will know," said Mum. "We'll take the tooth and the bone there. I think it's open late tonight. You're not going to leave your spinach, are you, Lucy? David's eaten his!"

Under the table, the dog licked a pile of slimy spinach out of David's hand.

"Let's get going then." David wiped off the flecks of green slobber on the dog's wiry coat and jumped to his feet.

"Come on, Popeye!" Lucy said. She clipped the dog's lead onto his collar.

"OK," said Mum. "The washing-up can wait. After all, we are on holiday."

They walked down the hill
towards the museum building.

"It's shaped like a pterosaur,"
David said. "That's the beak."

The pointed porch stood out
against the thundery sky.

The dog looked up and whimpered.

"I don't think he likes it," said Lucy.

"It's OK, Cowardy Custard," David said.

The dog pawed at Lucy and began to whine.

"Sorry," said Lucy. "You can't come inside." She tied the dog's lead to the bicycle rack. "Sit and stay! We won't be long."

They walked up to the
entrance desk.

"There's a Dinosaur Gallery!"
said Lucy, leafing through a
museum guidebook. "I can't
wait to see what's in there!"

"I'm very sorry," the lady at
the desk said. "It's closing time."

"But we have
something
to show
you."
David
held out the
tooth and the
bone.

"They're definitely fossils,"
said the lady, "but I'm not an
expert. Dr Simpson will be able
to tell you what they are
tomorrow."

"*Oooooooooow!*"

Outside, the dog was
howling.

"I'll buy the guidebook," said Mum. "We'll come back tomorrow without the dog."

"Look at this!" said Lucy. She pointed to a page at the back of the guidebook.

FREE ADMISSION FOR IDENTIFICATIONS

YOU MAY DISCOVER A NEW TYPE OF DINOSAUR!

Chapter Four

Whooooooooooooooooooosh! The caravan shook and the windowpanes rattled as the rain battered against them. Each time a gust of wind howled, the dog howled.

"*Ooooooooooooow!*"

"It's a wild night," Mum said.

"It's good weather for fossil-hunting," David said. "I bet we'll find lots tomorrow."

Lucy looked up from the museum guide she was reading.  "They call the Isle of Wight 'Dinosaur Isle', because of all the dinosaur fossils they've found here," she said. "There are photos of all sorts of fossils in this booklet. That's odd . . ."

Whooooooooooooosh! went the wind.

Oooooooow! went the dog.

Lucy raised her voice. "Miss Stone said our tooth was from a shark, but it looks more like a dinosaur tooth to me."

"Can't hear you," said David. "Be quiet, Noisy!"

The dog howled again.

"He's making terrible smells! We'd better take him out."

Mum pulled on her coat and picked up a torch. "Put the dog on the lead, David, and bring a poop-scoop bag. You'll have to come too, Lucy. I can't leave you here on your own. Walkies, Pongo!"

Whooooooooooosh!

The wind and the rain lashed across their faces as they walked towards the beach. Only a narrow strip of sand was untouched by the surging sea.

"The tide's very high," said Mum.

The dog put his nose down and started snuffling. Then he pricked up his ears and looked along the beach. A light was bobbing up and down near the base of the cliff. A torch light.

"I don't believe it!" Mum said. "Someone else is out on a wild night like this!"

The dog backed up, slipped his head out of his collar and disappeared into the darkness.

"Come here!" David, Lucy and Mum shouted all together.

Their voices were lost in the howling wind and the booming waves. A flash of lightning lit up the beach.

"He's running towards the person with the torch," David yelled. "Come on!"

"No!" Mum shouted. "We don't know who it is. The cliff's not safe. And the tide's coming in!"

Moonlight lit up the base of the cliffs.

"It's Miss Stone!" David said. "She's looking for something in the cliff."

"That's where the dog found the tooth and the bone," Lucy said. "The dog's jumping up at Miss Stone!"

"Look!" said Mum. "The cliff-face is moving!"

"Landslide!" they yelled. They watched in horror as a waterfall of mudstone flowed down the cliff towards the woman and the dog.

Thunderclouds rolled in front of the moon. The sky went dark. *Whump!* The ground shuddered as the landslip hit the beach.

"Oh no!" said Mum. "They'll be buried alive!"

Chapter Five

Another flash of lightning lit up the beach.

David, Lucy and Mum dashed towards the landslip.

Mum shone her torch on the
scene. On the edge of the
mudslide, near the bottom of the
cliff, a very muddy Miss Stone
was struggling to pull her feet
out of the mud. A very muddy
dog was scrabbling around
her ankles, barking madly.

Slurp. Miss Stone pulled her feet free. The dog stuck his nose down the hole where her feet had been and pulled something out.

His tail was wagging wildly.

"Are you OK?"

"I . . . I think so!" Miss Stone stuttered.

"Then let's get back to the caravan before we're cut off by the tide," Mum said.

They splashed through the surf. The dog trotted along proudly with his muddy trophy in his mouth.

"Whatever were you doing out there on a night like this?" Mum handed Miss Stone a mug of hot tea.

"I was checking the spot where your dog found that tooth." Miss Stone wrapped her hands around her mug. She looked shame-faced. "It's a dinosaur tooth. I don't have any dinosaur teeth in my collection. They're very rare.

I wanted to find one for myself.
I hoped the storm would wash
them out. It was stupid of me. I
got carried away."

"We found this bone as well."
Lucy handed it to Miss Stone.

"Part of a rib bone! And
what did your dog bring back
with him just now?"

The dog rummaged around
in his basket and picked up
something in
his mouth.

"Come
here!" said
David.

The dog
trotted over and sat at David's
feet.

"Drop!"

The dog dropped
a large
curved
stone at
their feet.

"It's a claw!" Miss Stone jumped up. "These could be bits of the same dinosaur.  There might be a whole skeleton in the cliff. We have to check it out!"

"Not now," said Mum. "The tide's too high. We'll go out at first light. You'd better sleep on the settee, Miss Stone. The dog will keep an eye on you and make sure you don't get carried away again."

The dog curled up at Miss Stone's feet and shut one eye. The other was fixed on Miss Stone.

"He'd make a good guard dog," said David. "Perhaps his name's Spike. Or Brutus . . . or Boris . . . or Gnasher . . . or Nipper, or . . ."

Chapter Six

As soon as it was light, an
excited dog dragged David
along the beach towards the
new landslip. Miss Stone, Mum
and Lucy struggled to keep up.

"*Ruff, ruff, ruff, ruff, ruff.*"

"What is it, boy?" David unclipped the dog's lead.

"*RUFF! RUFF! RUFF!*"

"Wow!" David gasped. The dog stood nose to nose with an enormous skull. The skull had two rows of vicious-looking fangs.

There was a gap where one had fallen out. David rummaged in his backpack and took out the tooth the dog had found. It fitted into the gap.

Beyond the skull was a scattering of huge bones. "A whole dinosaur!" breathed Lucy.

"We must call in the experts," said Miss Stone. "I'll go and wake up Dr Simpson. I know where he lives."

"Amazing . . ."

Dr Simpson peered over the top of his glasses and surveyed the scene. "And your dog discovered it, you say."

The dog pricked up his ears.

"That's right," said Lucy. "He's a fossil-hunter."

David took out the claw from his backpack and handed it to Dr Simpson.

"Amazing," Dr Simpson repeated. "This has to be the most complete skeleton of this type of dinosaur ever found!"

"What sort of dinosaur is it?" asked Lucy.

Dr Simpson took a stone and began to trace an outline in the sand.

BARYONYX

"It was a predator, with even more teeth and bigger claws than tyrannosaurus rex," he said. "The claw is the reason I can be so sure what sort of dinosaur this was. It's one of the biggest claws in the dinosaur world. In fact, some people even like to call this dinosaur 'Claws'.

Its proper name is baryonyx."

"*RUFF! RUFF! RUFF!
RUFF! RUFF!*"

"Look at the dog!" said
David. "He's quivering from
nose to tail!"

"He's excited!"
said Lucy.

"Me too!
Our dog
found a
dinosaur!"

"What
happens now?" asked Mum.

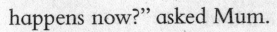

"We'll do a proper scientific
excavation," said Dr Simpson.

"If you come back next year, you should be able to see the skeleton in the museum. We'll put up a sign to say your dog found it. What's his name?"

"We're still trying to find out," said Mum.

David patted the dog's head.

THIS SKELETON WAS FOUND BY . . . . ?
(DAVID + LUCY'S DOG !)

"He's pleased that there will be a sign to say he found this bary— What did you call it? Baryonyx? Claws . . .?"

"RUFF! RUFF! RUFF! RUFF! RUFF!" The dog bounced up and down, barking.

"You must have said his name!" said Lucy.

The dog chased his tail round and round in circles.

"What, Claws? Cool!" said David.

The dog put his ears back. He lay down and whimpered.

"Not Claws," said Lucy. "Baryonyx!"

"*Ooooooooooooooowwwwwww,*"
the dog howled.

"No, not Baryonyx," said
David. "No one would call a
dog Baryonyx. Ba . . .
Barry . . ."

"*RUFF! RUFF! RUFF!
RUFF! RUFF!*"

". . . his name is Barry! That's
right, isn't it,
boy?"

The
dog
rolled
over and
over with joy.

"Barry! It's a terrific name for a dog that found a baryonyx!" Dr Simpson said.

"Barry!" David tickled the dog's warm tummy. "It's lucky you found a baryonyx, or we'd still be trying to work out your name!"

THE END

Also by Jane Clarke:

Only Tadpoles Have Tails,
illustrated by Jane Gray
Sherman Swaps Shells,
illustrated by Ant Parker

Also illustrated by
Garry Parsons:

Digging for Dinosaurs,
written by Judy Waite
Billy's Bucket,
written by Kes Gray